元曲選外編

第三冊

中華書局

differed, the action requested did not. We looked with particular interest at the proportion of section 136 requests made in relation to Afro-Caribbean people in view of other recent findings (Rogers and Faulkner, 1987) about the disproportionate use of police powers with black people. However, only 1.2 per cent of assessment requests relating to Afro-Caribbean people were for section 136, a marginally smaller proportion than for white people (1.3 per cent) and Asians (1.9 per cent) referred for this section. The proportion of emergency (section 4) requests was also smaller for Afro-Caribbeans, although the differences amounted to no more than 0.4 per cent.

Do we assume that because the rate of referral is considerably higher in the case of Afro-Caribbeans that they experience mental disorder at a higher rate than white people? Conversely, is mental disorder that much rarer amongst the Asian population? We have already discussed the danger of leaping to these sorts of conclusions in response to the comparative figures of men and women referred under the Mental Health Act. Stresses associated with migration, racism, social and economic disadvantage, and cultural change may well be understandable sources of poor mental health, which could account for a higher incidence of mental disorder amongst the non-white population. But why then is there such a difference between black Afro-Caribbean and black Asian people? Once again we have to look beyond this current study to understand the differences we have observed that need to be understood, not simply in terms of the characteristics that may be inherent in different groups, but in terms of the way in which behaviours and meanings are socially defined. 'One cannot understand mental illness in ethnic minorities by looking only at the patients' (Littlewood and Lipsedge, 1982:35).

Current psychiatric practice and concepts of mental disorder in the UK have been defined within the context of Western European cultures. Moreover, the time at which psychiatry was developing its respectability as a discipline within medicine was the time at which western imperialism was at its height. It would have been surprising if psychiatry had not been affected by those ideas of racial superiority on which economic and cultural imperialism were based. One example of this in practice was a belief, recently current, that African peoples did not experience depression as this was a malady that presupposed a mature and sophisticated mind.

The contention was that the simple nature of the Negro who gave little thought to the future and who made little distinction between himself and the outside world meant that depression was rare (Fernando, 1986).

Schizophrenia, however, *is* frequently identified as a malady experienced by black people. In this study, 74 per cent of the Afro-Caribbean men and 66 per cent of the Afro-Caribbean women were diagnosed as schizophrenic, a finding that reflects the diagnoses of people admitted to psychiatric hospitals or wards (Cochrane, 1983) and a number of other studies that have compared rates of identified mental illness. For example, Little-wood and Lipsedge quote findings that show that psychoses are diagnosed twice as often as neuroses amongst English men and internal immigrants, five or six times as frequently amongst Asians and European immigrants and *sixteen* times as frequently amongst West Indian immigrants.

This differential rate of diagnosis of different types of disorder is one indication of different perceptions of the behaviour of different ethnic groups that could affect the rate of referral. Rogers and Faulkner in their study of the use of section 136 have suggested that in removing Afro-Caribbean people from public places under this power, the police were often responding to the concern of the general public. Littlewood and Lipsedge note that behaviour that does not break the law is not a reason for referring someone to the public agencies, unless the individual concerned is actually perceived to be in danger themselves:

> Behaviour characterized by physical violence, assaults or destruction of property (that is to say deviant behaviour of an *overactive* rather than *underactive* type) is likely to lead to help being sought: the community cannot attempt to cope with this behaviour as they might with depression and withdrawal.
>
> (Littlewood and Lipsedge, 1982:74)

This may provide some explanation for the higher rate of referral of Afro-Caribbean people and also for the different referral routes, but it still leaves the question of why there should be such a high rate of diagnosis of schizophrenia. This is partly to do with the differences in the age structure of the different groups referred – over 40 per cent of the Afro-Caribbean people referred were under 25 compared with 13 per cent of the white people. But we also suspect that there may be an element of stereotyping at work. Husband notes how mugging has been stereotyped as a crime primarily committed by black youths and how 'We are not equally open to evidence on the characteristics of different people we meet; rather we are selectively cued to identify behaviour that fits our preconceived expectations' (Husband, 1986:6). Littlewood and Lipsedge suggest that identification of the two types of deviance may be linked:

> Black Britons are over-represented both in the diagnosis of schizophrenia and in certain patterns of crime. Are they placed in two deviant categories because of two different types of behaviour, or are the two linked? Are blacks perceived as both madder and badder than whites?
>
> (Littlewood and Lipsedge, 1982:199)

The only indirect evidence we have to offer in relation to this is in the different outcomes of assessment requests.

Whilst the general nature of the requests made to ASWs for assessments of different ethnic groups was largely similar, the outcomes of those requests were not. Overall, Afro-Caribbean people were most likely of all ethnic groups to be compulsorily detained following assessment. In view of their higher referral rate it is not surprising that they have been found to be disproportionately represented in the compulsorily detained psychiatric hospital population (Ineichen *et al.*, 1984). In our study they were also least likely to enter hospital informally *and* to receive alternative forms of care. The comparative rates of compulsory detention following all assessments were: 64.4 per cent of Afro-Caribbeans, 57.2 per cent of Asians, and 56.6 per cent of white people referred. If we separate out these figures according to the nature of the assessment request, the differences become even more noticeable: 80 per cent of Afro-Caribbean people referred for assessment under the emergency section were compulsorily detained compared with less than 59 per cent of white and Asian people; 78.8 per cent of section 2 assessments of Afro-Caribbeans resulted in compulsory detention compared with 68.7 per cent and 66.7 per cent of assessments of white and Asian people respectively. None of the Afro-Caribbean people assessed under section 4 entered hospital informally, although 21.6 per cent of white people and 16.7 per cent of Asian people did so and we have commented previously on the generally higher diversion rate following emergency assessment requests. The proportion of informal admissions following section 2 assessments for Afro-Caribbeans was almost half that of informal admissions of white and Asian people. They were also less likely to receive alternative care following both section 2 and section 4 assessments. The picture following assessment for section 3 is rather different: 82.7 per cent of Afro-Caribbeans were detained compulsorily compared with 80 per cent of Asian people but 88.3 per cent of white people. Their rate of informal admission was also higher than that of white people and they were more likely to receive alternative care than were both of the other groups. Compulsory detention following 'not specified' requests was highest for Afro-Caribbeans, but the differences were not as great. Asian people were least likely to be compulsorily detained following these non-specific assessments (see Table 6.5).

Table 6.5 Outcomes by section by ethnic group

	Compulsory admission	Informal admission	Alternative care
Section 2			
White	68.7	14.2	10.8
Afro-Caribbean	78.8	7.2	5.3
Asian	66.7	14.3	14.3
Section 3			
White	88.3	7.1	2.7
Afro-Caribbean	82.7	7.7	7.7
Asian	80	10	5
Section 4			
White	58.9	21.6	14.9
Afro-Caribbean	80.0	0	12.0
Asian	58.3	16.7	25
Not specified			
White	17.9	18.6	35.0
Afro-Caribbean	21.8	19.2	24.4
Asian	13.5	13.6	22.7

This is convincing evidence of a different experience according to ethnic group. It also emphasizes the necessity of distinguishing between different black groups when analysing and trying to understand the nature of that experience. We do not know what went on when ASWs were assessing any of the people referred during the course of this study. We do not know whether there was any direct or indirect expression of racism on the part of the workers concerned. But we can say that the cumulative effect of decisions made by those workers is indicative of a racist response to the mental health problems of those referred to them. As we noted in the section on gender, social workers are contributing to the definition of what is mental disorder whenever they make a decision that someone should or should not be detained under the Act. They are also defining which groups need to be admitted to hospital in order to receive care or treatment and which groups can receive such care and treatment in a less restrictive setting. On both counts there was a strong suggestion that more restrictive forms of 'care and treatment' were being considered appropriate in responding to the needs of people of Afro-Caribbean origin.

This finding from our study supports evidence from elsewhere. Aggrey Burke comments on a virtual lack of psychotherapy for blacks and that 'Essentially the mental (social) control aspect of psychiatry is far more evident among blacks than mental illness treatment and mental health promotion aspects, which instead are predominant white concerns' (Burke, 1986:151). Other evidence has pointed to more frequent recourse to compulsory detention of black people diagnosed as psychotic compared with both British born and white immigrants; although they are less likely to see their GP for psychiatric reasons, West Indian men have been found to be more likely to be admitted to psychiatric hospital; Asian-born patients have been found to be more likely to be involuntary patients and less likely to refer themselves; once in hospital and allowing for differences in diagnosis, black patients have been found to receive, more frequently, powerful phenothiazine drugs and ECT than white patients (quoted in Littlewood and Lipsedge, 1982). More recently the Mental Health Act Commission has commented on the lack of regular data collection to provide reliable information on the numbers of patients compulsorily detained from different ethnic groups. However, the Commission has been convinced by one-off studies and by evidence obtained from commissioners' visits that there is reason for concern at the over-representation of Afro-Caribbean people in compulsory hospital detention (Mental Health Act Commission, 1987).

Alongside the more frequent resort to the controlling aspects of the welfare state, we have to pose evidence about more limited access to caring services. The limitations of statutory social services in responding appropriately to the needs of black people is not confined to mental health services, (see, for example, Cheetham, 1981, Lewando-Hundt and Grant, 1987), but their failure in relation to mental health services may carry with it particularly severe implications both because of the too easy association between mental disorder and criminality, and because of the overt risk of deportation suffered by certain black patients admitted to hospital under the Mental Health Act (section 86: Removal of Aliens).

When hospital admission was avoided there were differences in the frequency with which different alternative resources were used. Family support and support from social workers were used most frequently in relation to the three groups, but the GP was a less frequent source of support to black people diverted from hospital admission. Somewhat surprisingly, in view of the high proportion of referrals of Asian people from GPs, support from the family doctor was used in less than 10 per cent of cases in which hospital admission was avoided. In contrast, the support of community psychiatric nurses was seen to be an appropriate resource in a higher proportion of incidents involving black people. Neither residential nor domiciliary care was ever used as an alternative to hospital admission for either Afro-Caribbean or Asian people and there was only one recorded use of day care and one of day hospital services. Voluntary support appeared to be more important for Afro-Caribbean and Asian people, and other not-specified resources were used more frequently with both Afro-Caribbean and Asian people. Whilst we do not know exactly what this involved, it may be that in the absence of appropriate statutory services a variety of voluntary, self-help, religious, or other specialist resources may have been used. (See Appendix 6 for more details of alternatives used.) Social workers thought the admission of both Afro-Caribbean and Asian people could have been prevented proportionately more often than in the case of white people. But the differences were small, and in the case of Afro-Caribbean people, would not go very far to close the gap in proportions of admissions. The comparative proportions of possible diversions were: 24.1 per cent – white, 25 per cent – Afro-Caribbean, and 27.1 per cent – Asian.

The range of statutory resources drawn on to avoid hospital admission was more limited in relation to both black groups, although the numbers of people involved were considerably smaller and this in itself would affect resource use. However, the picture in relation to further social work input regardless of the assessment outcome shows that Asian and Afro-Caribbean people referred were more likely to receive continuity of input from the social worker undertaking the assessment than were white people. The proportion of each group receiving 'no further action' was only marginally different.

The picture our project has painted generally in relation to continuity of service and the availability of well-developed community mental health resources is not a very positive one. In view of what we have already said about the greater range of resources generally available for elderly people in comparison to young people, it is not surprising that the picture is particularly negative for primarily young Afro-Caribbean people with mental health problems. The lack of appropriate resources designed particularly with the needs of this group in mind is likely to inhibit social workers' confidence about the possibilities of diversion. But the creation of appropriate resources depends in part on demands being made for them and whilst the perception is that a more coercive response is more frequently the right one, the pressure to develop appropriate responses will be lacking.

Origins of mental distress and implications for assessment

The onus on the social worker providing mental health assessments is to identify mental distress and the potential causes of it, which may be located in social and interactional factors that they may be able to do something about. They also need to be able to identify when there are situations in which other types of intervention would be appropriate. Littlewood and Lipsedge provide an example of this that makes no reference to race. They quote the example of two women, one hallucinating white mice, the other saying she was seeing visions of her dead husband:

If we encourage the woman with delirium tremens to talk about her hallucinations without offering her physical treatment, we will probably soon kill her, while to give drugs to the widow rather than help her to mourn her husband would be, at the best, grossly insensitive.

(Littlewood and Lipsedge, 1982:111)

There is an opposite tendency amongst professionals working with black people with mental health problems to the coercive response discussed earlier. That is either not to recognize mental distress expressed in physical symptoms, or to define 'abnormal' behaviour as 'normal' within an unfamiliar cultural context.

> A mental health team leader in an inner city SSD tells of an Asian woman, neglected by the husband she had lately followed to Britain, who developed paralysing pains down one side of her body. Her G.P. could only prescribe massive doses of analgesics. When her behaviour became more and more disruptive, it was left to the ASW to search out the emotional sources of her illness.
>
> (Tonkin, 1987: 19)

Aggrey Burke (1986) describes the case of a young woman from Trinidad and Tobago who became unsettled after the birth of her child. She was referred to her GP by her family, who did not respond as her behaviour was seen to be 'cultural'. After she had destroyed all her furniture and was seen by her neighbours to be in a daze within her own, closed-in world, a psychiatrist was brought in. Again the response was that such behaviour was cultural. When matters deteriorated further, her child was taken into care.

There *are* differences in the way in which mental distress may be expressed by men and women of different ethnic groups. Those differences are mediated by different social and cultural experiences that may, for example, mean that medicalizing emotional distress by expressing it in physical symptoms is more acceptable. This probably accounts in large part for the lower overall referral rate of Asian people and the greater frequency of their referral from medical sources. But those different experiences also point to different origins of mental distress and these have to be seriously acknowledged by mental health professionals in both understanding behaviour and pointing to appropriate responses. A response based purely on cultural relativism is not morally acceptable by a worker concerned with care and treatment.

Social workers need to know how racism can affect the mental health of people subject to it. Fernando identifies racism as the most important influence on depression amongst black people in the UK: 'Depression . . . is the name for an experience of a

174

disturbed equilibrium in a human being where the symptoms form the interface between the individual and the outside world' (Fernando, 1986: 121). The social context of a person from a black or ethnic minority is defined by cultural difference, minority status, and racism. In this situation, negative or insecure perceptions of self-identity, the experience of loss associated with an inability to achieve aspirations, and a conditioned helplessness as a result of repeated exposure to experiences over which they have no control, can lead to severe depression. The importance of this in determining an appropriate response to black people experiencing such depression is described as follows:

> An awareness of what happens is important because the patient has to develop strategies to safeguard self-esteem; finding alternative sources of self pride may mean identifying with (for example) black movements, or finding models (to identify with) that do not represent the dominant racial groups.
>
> (Fernando, 1986:130)

Apparently deviant behaviour may be an adaptation to bolster self-esteem or self-identity. As a way of surviving in an unfriendly environment it may be 'sane' rather than 'mad' behaviour and if challenged without understanding could result in breakdown. Indeed, it may be appropriate for social workers to help black people experiencing depression to find positive models to boost their self-image.

As well as the impact racism can have on self-esteem amongst black people, there are also more practical effects that may well influence mental health. Unemployment amongst the Afro-Caribbean people in these ten authorities was even higher than amongst the white population: 84.7 per cent of Afro-Caribbean men and 67.8 per cent of Afro-Caribbean women were described as being unemployed compared with 61.8 per cent of white men and 39.6 per cent of white women. Less than 9 per cent of Afro-Caribbean men were in full-time employment. Afro-Caribbean men and women were much less likely to be owner-occupiers than white people. These factors are indicative of a higher degree of social deprivation amongst Afro-Caribbean people, which has been well documented elsewhere (e.g. Brown, 1984).

Afro-Caribbean women were more often single parents within the household than were their white or Asian peers: 18.8 per cent of Afro-Caribbean women were living only with children compared with 7.5 per cent of white women and 3.2 per cent of Asian women. The proportion of men in this situation was negligible in all groups. Littlewood and Lipsedge (1982) comment that a high proportion of patients with acute psychotic reactions are single mothers struggling to bring up their children in adverse conditions. The stresses of unemployment, low income, poor housing, and lone parenthood will be compounded by the stresses of structural and overt racism and increase the likelihood of mental distress.

The differences in both referral rates and routes between Afro-Caribbean and Asian people have already been noted. There were also considerable differences in the characteristics and circumstances of the two groups. The greater youth of the Afro-Caribbean population is accompanied by differences in their marital status and living group. Only 6.2 per cent of Afro-Caribbean men were married, 38 per cent of them were living with their parents, and a similar percentage were living alone. In contrast, 53.6 per cent of Asian men were married, nearly 46 per cent were living with their partner, and only 12.9 per cent were living alone. In both black groups the proportion of men within the referred population was higher than the proportion of women. This represents an important difference between both black groups and the white people referred. One explanation of the gender differences amongst the Afro-Caribbean population may be the perceived dangerousness of the young Afro-Caribbean male to which we have already alluded. Whilst Afro-Caribbean women were more likely to be married than were the men, Asian women were somewhat less likely to be married than were Asian men. In consequence, they were the only group where the women were less likely to be living with a partner than were the men. Yet the comparison across ethnic groups shows that a higher proportion of Asian women were living with a partner than either white or Afro-Caribbean women.

Other important differences were indicated by the fact that of all groups, Asian people were most likely to be owner-occupiers and least likely to be council tenants and Asian men were more often in full-time employment than either white or Afro-Caribbean men. The Asian women were employed as often as white women, but less frequently than Afro-Caribbean women.

Finally, differences were also evident in the type of disorder experienced as determined by the psychiatric diagnosis. The predominance of schizophrenia diagnosed amongst Afro-Caribbean people means that it is difficult to make comparisons in relation to other disorders. However, some characteristics do stand out. Asian men were given a diagnosis of affective psychosis more often than any other group of either men or women, and the proportion of Asian women with a diagnosis of depression was higher than the proportion of white women and four times as high as the proportion of Afro-Caribbean women with this diagnosis (see Figure 6.2)

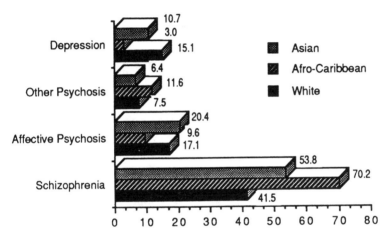

Figure 6.2 A comparison of diagnosis by ethnic group

All these factors have implications for the social worker undertaking assessments of people referred to them because their mental disorder is causing concern. The Asian people referred can be seen as least likely to be marginal in terms of their socio-economic circumstances. This may itself reflect certain character-istics of the Asian population as a whole. The importance of the family as both a reproductive unit and as the primary source of support and interdependence is greater amongst the Asian than the white population (Anwar, 1986). Mental disorder will be con-tained within the family as the primary responsibility for dealing with problems is seen to be the responsibility of the family itself. Yet the disruption of the total family unit that may have been the result of emigration can mean that the particular members of the family who would have provided support are not immediately available. Women living in their husband's family may not have access to their own families to provide support at times of conflict (Bravington and Majid, 1986; Fernando, 1986; Littlewood and Lipsedge, 1982). Intergenerational conflict resulting from the experience of growing up in a very different cultural environment can mean that family relationships are a source of stress that may contribute to mental health problems. The assumption that the extended family can always provide the care that Asian women with mental health problems need has been regarded as racial stereotyping that absolves professionals from fulfilling their responsibilities (Malik, n.d.) In fact family support was less often used as an alternative to prevent hospital admission of Asian people than it was with Afro-Caribbean or white people, although social workers identified such support as required to avoid 'preventable' admissions slightly more often – in 37.9 per cent of cases involving Asian people and 35.8 per cent of cases involving white people.

Isolation caused by language difficulties provides another dimension to the mental health difficulties of Asian people in Britain. This is particularly acute for women, many of whom have been in the UK for a much shorter time than men (Henley, 1986). A study by Brown (1984) showed that 76 per cent of Bangladeshi women, 70 per cent of Pakistani women, and 42 per cent of Indian women in the UK could speak little or no English. The accurate communication of feelings of mental distress is highly dependent on shared language and meanings. By the time someone is assessed by a social worker for possible compulsory detention, they may already have had the experience of failing to communicate adequately with other professionals. Malik quotes an example of failure to communicate even though an interpreter was available:

> Mrs J, an elderly Pakistani woman was the victim of a fraud case. She had been robbed of all her money. Since this incident she had withdrawn completely and refused verbal communications.
>
> An interpreter was used during Mrs J's assessment. The assessment lasted half an hour.

Question: What did you manage to convey during the assessment?
Answer: Just the facts of what happened to her.
Question: Was that all you managed to convey?
Answer: Yes. I asked her ten questions and received one answer. I asked her another ten questions and got only one answer again. I could only convey what had made her withdraw and not how she felt.

(Malik, n.d. :14)

Withdrawal is an understandable reaction when communication is difficult but can lead to further isolation and depression. Bravington and Majid point to another response available to people who cannot understand what is going on around them; that of observing what others are doing and copying them. They point out that in a psychiatric ward this can lead to further complications. We were not able to collect information on the ethnic origin of social workers carrying out assessments under the Act. But our impression is that few authorities employ sufficient bilingual ASWs to ensure that language is not a problem whenever they interview non-English speaking people 'in a suitable manner' (section 13.2) to determine whether or not they should be compulsorily detained.

Considerable understanding and sensitivity is required from ASWs who may be asked to assess people of different cultures and who have had experiences of racism that they can never share. Particularly in those areas in which there is a large black population the appointment of Afro-Caribbean and Asian ASWs should be a priority, but the responsibilities of white ASWs in this area should also be acknowledged by appropriate training. Whilst we recognize that individual actions alone cannot overcome the structural racism evident in the mental health system as in other systems and organizations within our society, the actions of social workers should not reinforce a racist, stereotyped interpretation of human behaviour.

The black Briton has the same problems of every day life as the white: economic security, a satisfactory personal and professional life and the need to make sense of his existence. His problems are, however, continually refracted through the experience of racism. Psychiatry continually reinforces this

179

flawed identity by its concern with the individual rather than the social and by its readiness to accept as primary the reflections thrown into it by other social phenomena.

(Littlewood and Lipsedge, 1982:239)

This sexist analysis of basic needs nevertheless has an important point to make. We have already argued that social work takes place at the interaction between the individual and the social and that the ASW should challenge psychiatric definitions when they fail to acknowledge the social construction of behaviour. Our results in relation to the different outcomes for different ethnic groups suggest that social work, too, is reinforcing 'this flawed identity'.

Chapter 7

BEYOND SECTIONING

In the past, Mental Welfare Officers talked about 'doing a section' when they were called on to undertake their responsibilities in relation to the mental-health legislation. Such an expression implies an assumption that the social worker was there merely to ensure procedures were followed once the doctors involved had reached a decision about the need for someone to be compulsorily detained in hospital. Disagreements did occur and admission did not always take place, but the terminology used by workers served to minimize their potential role in providing a different perspective on mental distress based on a particular expertise in understanding behaviour rather than illness.

We do not know whether there has been any change in the frequency of disagreement between referrer and social worker following the implementation of the 1983 Act and the enhanced recognition it gave to the role of the social worker. There *has been* a change in terminology: workers talk of doing assessments more often than they used to. But if one of the aims of the 1983 Act was to promote the social perspective on mental disorder to a position alongside the medical and legal perspectives, we feel this was insufficiently articulated within the framing of the Act itself, and doomed to failure without more far-reaching changes alongside the legislative recasting. We feel this reflects a high degree of uncertainty amongst workers in social services departments who may represent the only institutional and professional guardians of an alternative perspective, but who have failed to build an alternative practice that can provide a forceful and credible alternative to medical treatment.

Social services departments find it hard to define who the

mental health client group actually is. In administrative terms, a single adult may become a 'mental health case' by default: they are not in a family, not elderly, and with no obvious physical or mental handicap. Conversely, a severely depressed young mother is likely to be defined as a 'family case' and an elderly man with dementia is likely to be categorized as 'elderly'. They are not alone in this difficulty. The medical profession finds considerable difficulty in agreeing amongst itself when people are suffering from particular conditions, like schizophrenia, and whether in fact there is any one condition 'schizophrenia' which can be defined in ways other than describing symptoms. The legislators, too, failed to provide explicit criteria to determine to whom the Act was intended to refer:

> Section 1 (2) In this Act – '"mental disorder" means mental illness, arrested or incomplete development of mind, psychopathic disorder and any other disorder or disability of mind and "mentally disordered" shall be construed accordingly.

Whilst they go on to define 'severe mental impairment', 'mental impairment', and 'psychopathic disorder', they provide no definition of 'mental illness'.

The definition of the term mental illness is thus left to those to whom the legislators ascribe the responsibilities for putting the legislation into practice: primarily doctors and approved social workers. In discussing our findings and their possible interpretation, we have thus had to explore concepts of mental health, their origins, and institutionalization that will affect those definitions. Since our concern is with the implementation of the Act by social services, our major focus has been on the historical neglect of the social dimension in mental health policy and what this means for the definitions that social workers are able to offer and the responses they are able to make.

Our analysis has been critical of the performance of social services in this area. This is not intended as negative criticism. We are arguing for the role of social services in the provision of mental health services and in the application of the legislation to be given at least equal prominence to the medical role. But if this is to be achieved it will require considerable resource and practice development within the context of coherent policy and adequate resourcing at both national and local level. As in any change in the balance of power it will require some power to be given up particularly over the control of resources, and the preparedness elsewhere to recognize a level of responsibility not previously evident. What follows is an attempt to locate some of the changes that would be implied.

HOSPITAL OR COMMUNITY?

The bulk of spending on mental health services goes on hospital services. Treatment in hospital is seen to be an appropriate way of responding to problems caused by illness. Being 'ill' is more respectable than being 'mad' and the pre-eminence of the hospital as the dominant treatment site is thus reinforced by some people with mental disorder and by their carers. But would that attitude remain if opportunities for treatment in all its forms were equally available within the community?

We have seen that a higher proportion of elderly people are diverted from hospital admission than are other groups and we have explained this by the greater availability of community-based resources for elderly people. The responsibility to provide a range of resources that can provide personal, social, and practical care for elderly people to enable them to continue living in their own homes when this would not be possible without help, is well accepted. So, too, is the responsibility to provide alternative accommodation if intensive support at home is inappropriate or insufficient. The same responsibilities are not so readily accepted in relation to people whose problems of self-care derive from mental health problems rather than age.

We have quoted research that demonstrates as good if not better outcomes from care and treatment provided within the community compared with hospital-based treatment. We have also referred to research that identifies social problems that can contribute to the development of mental disorder. These are two strong but different arguments for the need to develop community-based mental health resources. The first suggests people should have the right to choose between different responses to their problems if those responses are equally efficacious in promoting improvement. The second point implies that if at least some causes of mental disorder can be located in the social system within which the individual lives, then the 'cure' should be either in changing aspects of that system or enabling the person concerned to limit its disabling effects. Many of the problems dealt with by the mental health services are simply problems of living: most have structural dimensions – problems of poverty, housing, unemployment, marginalization, racism, and sexism, whilst others may be more conventionally thought of as relationship problems. Solutions to those problems are not within the grasp of any one professional or any one professional group, but response to the individual consequences of such structural problems has been seen to be the particular province of social work – both through case work and through the mobilization of other practical and therapeutic resources.

Community care as policy and practice is considerably less developed in mental health services than in mental handicap services. It is currently uncertain whether the identification of social services departments' key responsibility in identifying and assessing need in the *Griffiths Report* (Griffiths, 1988) will result in any retargetting of resources towards community care in general and community mental health services in particular. The difference between mental health and mental handicap services lies in the much greater agreement both within social services and between social and health services about both the values and the objectives to be achieved. Thus the discussion of how to make progress in the development of community resources is tied up with the need to achieve greater clarity in relation to concepts of mental health and the reasons for its breakdown. As long as the dominant concept is that of 'illness', social services are going to be unlikely to be able to argue convincingly that the necessarily professional expertise is available amongst their staff.

One concern arising from our analysis of our research findings is that social services staff themselves have a tendency to defer to psychiatric explanations and responses. Rather than drawing on their particular understanding of individual behaviour in a social context, they may be too ready to borrow the language of psychiatry to describe rather than explain behaviour. This is understandable in view of the content of approved social worker training (discussed in Chapter 5), which is a further symptom of the undeveloped state of practice in relation to mental health work. Consideration is currently being given to the content of refresher training for ASWs and there is at least some acknowledgement of the need to develop understanding and awareness of specific factors: gender, age, ethnic group, as well as the need for 'well-rounded social work assessment' of people assessed under the Act.

Development of individual skills is one requirement in promoting a valuable social response to mental disorder, but this will be insufficient if individual practice is expected to take place within an unchanged organizational environment. The intensive work involved in organizing and maintaining social networks that can support people experiencing severe mental distress will not be possible so long as it has to compete for space with work with children and families given priority by statutory requirements and moral panic. This is not an argument for mystifying and separating mental health work into a distinct specialism. Our argument is that the basis for the development of such approaches lies within more general social work understanding and skills. But the organization of work may well require change and this requires a clarity about policy and purpose amongst those responsible for planning and managing mental health social services that was not often evident in responses to the questionnaire sent to departments participating in this study. We have to recognize that radical shifts in priorities and resourcing within social services from child care to mental health are neither likely nor desirable. Yet we also need to reiterate that concern with child care problems that does not recognize or address their origins (where this applies) in mental health problems of parents, will often lead to lengthy and unproductive involvement with families where problems are not solved because underlying causes are not addressed. One strategy that has shown some indications of success in a small-scale experiment (see Maple, 1988) has involved a sharing of responsibilities between workers; one concerned with child care issues, the other addressing explicitly the mental health problems of the parent. But Maple's work again highlighted the fact that mental distress was often not explicitly acknowledged by social workers (see also Cohen and Fisher, 1987) and this emphasizes the need for a broadening rather than a narrowing of understanding and involvement in mental health work within social services departments.

Consideration of the future role of social services in relation to mental health legislation has to be seen within the context of how they view their responsibilities to the much larger number of

185

people experiencing mental distress who are never made subject to that legislation. This is evident from the apparent randomness with which people come to be considered for possible action under the Act in some parts of the country compared with others. We could find no apparent link between the proportion either assessed or detained with either population size or other characteristics of the area. We were left to conclude that it was the policy and practice of health and social services authorities themselves that most affected the likelihood of referral under the legislation. It is our view that the lack of a clear policy in relation to mental health services generally can have a net-widening effect in relation to involvement in the legislation for two reasons. First, the lack of 'preventive' resources may mean crises arise that would not otherwise have done so, or are indeed 'manufactured' as the only way in which it is possible to obtain a response. Second, unfamiliarity with working with people whose behaviour is bizarre and apparently difficult to understand may result in an over-response. It is worthy of note that the authority in our study with the most clearly articulated crisis intervention service had one of the lowest rates of detention. We have emphasized the need to be cautious about equating high levels of diversion with good practice, or assuming that high diversion in itself is indicative that people with mental health problems are receiving a 'good' service. Diversion in many instances is likely to have meant that family and friends will have continued to provide support and assistance, often with very limited input from social services. Unless SSDs have both clear policies and resources that enable them to provide continuing support for people who may on occasion be considered for hospital admission, their practice at the time of assessment may feel largely irrelevant to people experiencing mental health problems and those who usually care for them.

We do not consider it is appropriate for us to advocate one particular model that should be adopted by all SSDs in relation to their mental health services. We have no evidence from our study of what such a model would look like. The evidence we do have indicates a need for clarity of purpose and for the development of services which are appropriate for the particular local population. We also consider that there is no purpose in social services departments trying to export institutional, medical models of mental health: there is much to be learnt from community mental handicap teams that have clearly articulated a non-medical, non-institutional approach to services.

Whatever model or organization is adopted, it should have certain characteristics. It should allow psychiatry as control of deviant behaviour to be challenged. There is a considerable contradiction between the stance of the state in purporting to enact legislation to protect its members even from themselves when at the same time the very minimum ingredients of 'social security' are not provided to many of its members. The unequal identification of mental disorder amongst different groups with those groups most powerless in social and economic terms also being those most stigmatized by being labelled mentally ill is not coincidence. The developing strengths of groups of mental health service users (e.g. Barker and Peck, 1987) are indicative of the importance of being able to take control of your own life in recovering mental health. Attempting to impose patterns of behaviour that society regards as 'normal' for people in particular circumstances, but which are experienced as stressful by the person concerned, is not an appropriate response from an agency that should be promoting the social perspective on mental health. In individual practice, and in policy and resourcing, social services should be challenging sexist, ageist, and racist stereotyping, which contribute to the imbalance in experience of the mental health system. They should also not require a person to submit to treatment based on intrapsychic theories of causation (see Banton *et al.*, 1985) when the causes of stress and distress are to be found in structural factors.

This is not to deny or ignore the very real individual pain felt and the need to offer personal help to distressed people. But there should perhaps be a degree of humility on the part of those working in the mental health services in recognition of the continuum of personal experience between those helping and those helped: the language and practice of so-called 'professionals' needs to change to reflect this continuum rather than becoming more technically daunting and mystifying with the aim of putting immediate misery at safe distance. Above all, this implies a readiness both to listen to and to take seriously the description of what the experience of mental disorder means to the person concerned. What being mentally ill feels like and how it affects behaviour may be more important in determining what an appropriate response should be than trying to arrive at an accurate diagnosis. A typical outcome of mental disorder is a lowering of self-esteem and confidence (see, for example, Ritchie *et al.*, 1988), which contributes to further isolation and marginalization. Criticisms of medical treatment that responds to the symptoms or disorder, but fails to recognize the individual as a person are too frequent to be ignored. People experiencing mental health problems often recognize the contribution that medication can make to easing their immediate pain (Ritchie *et al.*, 1988, Bailey, 1987) but if this is not accompanied by counselling, attendance to practical questions of where they live, what they are able to do with their time, their financial circumstances, and their need for companionship and emotional support, medication is likely to become a long-term prop rather than a means to resolve difficulties.

It is something of a cliché to say that collaboration between professionals with different knowledge and skills is necessary to ensure that appropriate help is offered at appropriate times. Nevertheless, we have to repeat it here because of the continuing failure to achieve such interdisciplinary working in practice. Booth *et al.*, (1985) have commented on the failure of collaboration due to obstacles at operational and strategic levels that have resulted in people being compulsorily admitted to hospital when this could have been avoided. We have commented on more than one authority in our study with comparatively successful records in avoiding detention in which there is evidence of joint working between social workers and psychiatrists. Collaboration between health and social services in community mental health provision is being developed (see McAusland, 1985) and initial indications are that outcomes of such collaboration are positive. But a social response to the needs of mentally disordered people must also involve liaison with housing, recreational, and employment services if the total range of needs are to be met.

A social response to the needs of mentally disordered people should also be able to provide asylum. Once again, people who have experienced the disabling effects of mental disorder are clear that there are times when the need to retreat from the stresses of daily life and be cared for is pre-eminent. What they are less happy about is the way in which that care is currently provided. The concept of asylum has an important place within community mental health services, but its practical expression needs to be varied. The frequency with which alternative residential accommodation was mentioned as a resource to prevent hospital admission is probably not so much an expression of a need for long-term change in the home (although this might at times be what is required) as an expression of a need for 'time out' and removal from the environment in which distress was being experienced.

It is appropriate for SSDs to provide crisis accommodation for people with mental health problems. It is also appropriate for them to provide a range of hostels and group homes with staff available to provide support, encouragement, and more specialized forms of therapy and social skills development. But social services departments are not and should not be housing agencies and longer term asylum could also involve assisting people to live in their own independent accommodation rather than providing accommodation themselves. Where residential care is provided directly by social services, this should be based on a positive approach to the benefits of collective living rather than as an inevitably second-rate solution. Such benefits can be experienced and appreciated spontaneously by those living collectively in less than ideal conditions. The availability of companionship as and when it was wanted was cited as one of the benefits of living in private hotels as well as by those living in staffed hostels in a survey of people who had two or more admissions to hospital for treatment of mental illness in Birmingham (Ritchie *et al.*, 1988). Our results suggest that the use of residential care should not be seen as a closed system. The provision of support within a controlled environment should not preclude the maintenance of links with the world outside in order to avoid the danger of further marginalization for the people concerned (see Davis, 1984 for a discussion of models of residential care appropriate in this context).

WHAT OF MENTAL HEALTH LEGISLATION?

If developments along the lines discussed above were to take place, the social response to those experiencing mental disorder would be promoted to a position in which it could challenge more effectively the ideological dominance of medicine in both diagnosis and response. This in itself would make much clearer the legal question of when it is acceptable to take over control of people's lives against their will. Unless protecting the interests of others, those referred for detention should be seen as already sufficiently marginalized and in need of actions that increase rather than reduce their social integration – an approach that we have described as creating or supporting social networks. This should be the specialist realm of the social workers, supported by the resources of the social services department. It should comprise the organization and management of social networks designed to increase the likelihood that they will support and tolerate people in distress, rather than reject them, aided rather than hindered by medical and nursing help, and aided rather than hindered by the legal framework. If a fully developed social response based on solid foundations of understanding, skills, and resources failed to ensure care and support for mentally disordered people whose behaviour represented a real threat to others then compulsory detention could be legitimated. As it is, legislation that is intended to ensure equal treatment for all those at whom its provisions are aimed, fails in this aim because it provides no rights to assistance and leaves too much scope to the influence of ideological and resource constraints. It also provides in some ways less rights than criminal legislation governing arrest and prosecution, and some may argue from this that the use of criminal law would provide more protection to people experiencing mental disorder than does welfare legislation.

Social welfare legislation embodies the state's ambiguous attitude towards welfare provision. There is no consensus about the state's role in providing social services as there is in the provision of education. This is one reason for the reluctance to pass and implement welfare legislation that focuses on the rights of individuals to have their needs assessed and services provided. It is significant that the major recent exception to this, the Disabled Persons (Services, Consultation and Representation) Act, 1986 started out as a Private Members Bill and at the time of writing there are still major sections for which no implementation date has been set. Acceptance of the centrality of the role of the state in providing adequately for the needs of its most disadvantaged members would have enormous resource implications. However, if there is to continue to be legislation that defines those circumstances in which the state, as represented by workers in health and welfare services, can take control of people's lives when no crime has been committed, this *must* be balanced by legislation that gives rights to services that can prevent crises arising. Those experiencing severe mental health problems are poorly served by preventive and supportive services. The legislation defines those circumstances in which they can be compulsorily admitted to hospital and in which they can be given treatment against their will. If they are not admitted to hospital, legislation does not *require* the provision of alternative care, even though it acknowledges that 'care and treatment' may not always be appropriately provided by hospital admission.

We are left asking whether legislation can have a part to play in improving resources and altering the experience of those people with mental disorder who are brought within the mental health system. This has obviously been the case in Italy where Law 180, passed five years before the Mental Health Act, 1983, prohibits new admissions to psychiatric hospitals, prohibits the construction of new hospitals, and encourages the development of community care by strict adherence to the least restrictive alternative. The passage of the law was a response to changes being actively pursued by mental health workers who construed psychiatry as political activity. There are differences of opinion about the extent to which the Italian community mental health services have developed sufficiently to replace hospital services (see, for example, Jones and Polietti, 1985 and Ramon, 1983). Certainly developments have been varied in different parts of the country and changes in the system of mental health care itself cannot solve underlying problems of lack of housing and employment opportunities, which are important if people are to enjoy a full life in the community. However, the law forces attention to be shifted away from hospital care in a much more radical way than the rather half-hearted admonitions of the 1983 Act. Rather than relying on individual assessments of whether 'detention in a hospital is in all the circumstances of the case the most appropriate way of providing the care and medical treatment of which the patient stands in need' (section 13(2)), the Italian law is based on a *general* conclusion that such detention will not be the best way of providing care for people with severe mental health problems. The result is that unlike in the UK it would seem that at the cultural level, the psychiatric hospital is dead and buried (Ramon, 1988).

Whether legislation could have a similar impact in the UK is uncertain. There has never been a well-developed political awareness amongst opponents of orthodox psychiatry in this country and the Italian experience suggests that both awareness of the political dimensions of the mental health system as well as a political will to change would be necessary prerequisites for securing the radical legislation needed to bring about change.

Perhaps the most encouraging developments in this country are to be found in the growing user movement – achieving change from the 'bottom up' by working on changing relationships between users and mental health professionals.

In the context of legislation, which says virtually nothing about rights to services, it is not surprising that many of those who have become involved with mental health services against their will, regard themselves as 'recipients' or 'survivors' of the mental health system rather than users of a service. But the growth of patients' councils, the development of self-advocacy, and the establishment of Survivors Speak Out, partnership in providing services such as the Contact group in Chesterfield (see Barker and Peck, 1987) all demonstrate in different ways a gradual shift in the balance of power at the point at which services are delivered. In some cases these developments have taken place with allies amongst mental health professionals who have recognized that empowerment is an important step along the road to mental health. Whether this movement will achieve a groundswell sufficient to lead to legislative change or a change in the balance between medical and social perspectives on mental disorder is too soon to say. Our results have confirmed the distance to be travelled before such a change is achieved.

APPENDICES

APPENDIX 1

THE MENTAL HEALTH ACT 1983

This is not the place for a detailed account of the mental health legislation – the reader is referred to the introductory work of Gostin (1983) and the reference work of Hogget (1984). However, we are aware that at some points we assume familiarity with the teminology used in the legislation and we include brief explanations of some of the terms frequently employed in the text.

Approved social worker – a term introduced in section 114, meaning those workers approved by the local authority as 'having appropriate competence in dealing with those who are suffering from mental disorder'. At the time of the study, this meant workers who had either passed an examination prescribed by the Central Council for Education and Training in Social Work ('fully' approved for up to 5 years) or those who had undertaken a training course without examination ('transitionally' approved for up to 2 years). It is the ASW who normally makes the application for someone to be detained.

Mental disorder is the legal term used to cover mental illness, mental impairment, severe mental impairment, and psychopathy. Mental impairment refers to people with mental handicap who are judged to be 'abnormally aggressive' or 'seriously irresponsible'.

Mental Health Act Commission is a special health authority established under section 121 to exercise the powers of the Secretary of State to safeguard the interests of detained patients.

Mental Health Review Tribunal reports are required whenever a detained patient appeals to a tribunal against her or his detention or is automatically referred to one.

Nearest relative – the Act defines who may be classified as the nearest relative, because it is this person who has certain legal powers, including the power to make the application to have their relative detained.

Second opinions under sections 57/58 – the Act makes detailed provision for the compulsory treatment of those 'liable to be detained'. One safeguard is a second opinion from an independent medical practitioner that the treatment is necessary.This doctor is required to consult two other professionals and one is often a social worker.

'Sectioned' refers to the state of being subject to the compulsory powers available under the Mental Health Act, 1983.

Section 2 is the most widely used form of detention. It requires two medical recommendations and an application, may last for up to 28 days, and although described in the legislation as admission for 'assessment' may in fact be used to oblige someone to accept treatment.

Section 3 requires two medical recommendations and an application and may last for up to 6 months with options to renew for further periods. Although described as admission for 'treatment', this section does not in practice differ from admission under section 2 except in duration.

Section 4 is not, strictly speaking, a separate form of admission at all, but is an admission for assessment (under section 2) without one of the medical recommendations. It is intended for urgent cases where waiting for the second medical recommendation would involve 'undesirable delay'. On admission to hospital (for up to 72 hours), the obtaining of a second medical recommendation converts this into detention under section 2 without a further application by the ASW or nearest relative.

Section 7 (Guardianship) provides for the appointment of a guardian to exercise care and control over mentally disordered people short of admission to hospital. The guardian has three 'essential powers' to require the person to live in a specified place, to require the person to attend specified places 'for the purpose of medical treatment, occupation, education, or training', and to require access to be given to an ASW or a doctor.

Section 12 Doctor – the medical equivalent of the approved social worker. Psychiatrists are approved under section 12 but many GPs also act in this capacity.

Section 13 (4) provides that an ASW must assess a person for compulsory detention if requested to do so by their nearest relative.

Section 14 requires a social worker (not necessarily an ASW) to provide a social report on people compulsorily detained by reason of an application by their nearest relative.

Section 117 (Aftercare) – requires SSDs and Health Authorities, together with other agencies, to provide aftercare for patients who have been detained under section 3 and certain sections applying to patients convicted of criminal offences.

Section 136 provides powers to the police to remove to 'a place of safety' (usually a police station) anyone who 'appears to be suffering mental disorder and to be in immediate need of care or control'. The power lasts for up to 72 hours to allow an assessment by an ASW and a registered medical practitioner to be arranged.

WHAT WERE THE CRITERIA FOR INCLUSION OF A PIECE OF WORK IN THE STUDY?

The system of local implementation of the study through liaison researchers was intended to ensure a measure of consistency in the operation of the criteria for inclusion. The definition used was:

A form should be completed whenever the worker is requested to carry out or considers action under the Mental Health Act 1983.

Hence, inclusion depended on the worker's perception that a piece of work fell under the Act. Where requests concerned a specific section of the Act, relying on the worker's perception should have been unproblematic, and the accuracy of returns will have depended on local briefings about the project's remit. These should also have indicated that all requests for assistance with informal admission (defined as part of the ASW's role in DHSS circular LAC 83/7) were also to be included. Considerable concern was generated, however, about the comparability between authorities of the 25% of requests for ASW assessments where the likely outcome was not specified.

These were only to be included where action under the Act was seriously considered as part of the assessment process and many cases included in this category were simply of clear requests for compulsion to be applied where no specific section was cited. Indeed, a study of requests under the 1959 Act indicated that 43 per cent of requests to use compulsion failed to specify the section in this way (Fisher *et al.*, 1984).

None the less, there was considerable scope here for local interpretation and all these requests were scrutinized centrally. Where we felt doubt remained about the validity of their inclusion they were either rejected or returned to local liaison officers for further consideration of whether they should be included or not. Several hundred incidents were excluded in this way. At the end of this process we were happy that these requests were legitimately included in our data set. The only reservations that remained were over those possibly excluded at the local level because of too tight an interpretation of the project's remit but clearly there was little we could do about these and we had no way of estimating accurately the possible number. Those local checks that were carried out, however, suggested no major under-recording occurred of the incidents that were central to our interest.

APPENDIX 2

Table A2.1 Mental Health Act 1983 Monitoring Form

Social Services Department

Please see instructions on reverse

Referral date				Time		Client name	

Age		Male		Female		Worker	

Tick if any of these circumstances apply:

- ASW
- Intake Team Worker
- Hospital Team Worker
- Working out of hours/Standby/EDT
- Working outside normal locality

Formal marital status

- 0 Not known
- 1 Single
- 2 Married
- 3 Separated
- 4 Widowed
- 5 Divorced

Living group

- 00 Not known
- 01 Alone

Family

- 02 Spouse/Cohab only
- 03 Spouse/Cohab and children
- 04 Children only
- 05 Parents only
- 06 Siblings only
- 07 Parents and siblings
- 08 Parents, Spouse/Cohab
- 09 Parents, Spouse/Cohab and other family

Non-family

- 10 Non-relatives (incl. non-staffed group home)
- 11 NHS Unit
- 12 SSD Unit (staffed)
- 13 Private/vol. accommod.
- 14 Other (specify)

Action requested

- 01 ASW assessment: S.2
- 02 ,, : S.3
- 03 ,, : S.4
- 04 ,, : S.13(4)
- 05 ,, : S.136
- 06 ASW assessment: Guardianship S.7
- 07 Assistance with informal admission
- 08 Mental health assessment: action not specified
- 09 Social report (S.14) after S.2
- 10 Social report (S.14) after S.3
- 11 MHRT report after S.2
- 12 ,, S.3
- 13 MHRT report after S.37 (Hospital order)
- 14 Opinion re. treatment (S.57/58)
- 15 Aftercare S.117
- 16 Other (specify)

Employment

- 0 Not known
- 1 Full-time employment
- 2 Full-time care of home/family
- 3 Part-time employment
- 4 Unemployed
- 5 Retired
- 6 Full-time student
- 7 Other (specify)

Outcome

- 01 Advice given: contact
- 02 ,, : no contact
- 03 Application: S.2
- 04 ,, : S.3
- 05 ,, : S.4
- 06 Informal admission
- 07 Guardianship (S.7)
- 08 Report/treatment opinion/ aftercare given
- 09 SSD aftercare not available
- 10 Client declined aftercare
- 11 No application: informal in-patient status continued
- 12 No application: nearest relative application
- 13 No admission: alternative care
- 14 Other (specify)

Housing

- 0 Not known
- 1 Owner occupied
- 2 Private rented
- 3 Council/Housing Assoc.
- 4 Lodgings
- 5 Homeless/NFA
- 6 Other (specify)

Ethnic group

0	Not known	4	Mixed (specify)
1	White	5	Other (specify)
2	Afro-Caribbean		
3	Asian		

Psychiatric diagnosis

Has a diagnosis been made?

1 Yes   2 No   3 Don't know

If yes, specify diagnosis (if known) _____

If yes, by whom

1 GP   2 Psychiatrist   3 Both

Describe situation

Referred by

00	Not known
01	Self
02	Relative
03	Friend/Neighbour
04	Police/Courts
05	GP
06	Psychiatric in-patient service
07	Psychiatric out-patients' service
08	Housing
09	DHSS
10	Health Visitor
11	Social Services Depart.
12	Other (specify)

Case status at referral

1 New   2 Current open case

3 Other previous contact

Specify weeks since last contact

Alternatives to admission

	Required	Used
Family/Neighbour support		
Social Work intervention		
GP support		
Day Centre attendance		
Day Hospital attendance		
Domiciliary services		
Alternative residential accommodation		
Psychiatric out-patient help		
CPN help		
Crisis intervention team		
Voluntary agencies' help		
Other (specify below)		

Describe alternatives

Time worked (up to outcome)

	No.hrs
Contacts with client/family	
Contacts with others involved	
Internal consultation	
Records/Reports	

Further work

1 Retained by above worker

2 Referred to another worker/team

3 No further action

Date of completion of form

Departmental classification

INSTRUCTIONS FOR COMPLETION

1. The form should be completed by the worker who carried out the work requested as soon as possible after the outcome recorded under 'Outcome'. Where aftercare under S.117 has been requested, the form should be completed not later than 4 weeks after referral. The form requires you to tick the relevant box or to enter the relevant code in the box.

2. **Referral**   Please enter the date as follows – 27th March, 1984 becomes $\boxed{2\,|\,7\,|\,0\,|\,3\,|\,8\,|\,4}$

If the request for action concerns a currently open case, record the date of request

3. **Time**   Please use the 24-hour clock, so that 3.30 p.m. becomes $\boxed{1\,|\,5\,|\,3\,|\,0}$

4. **Client name**   This will not appear on the carbon sent for processing.

5. **Formal marital**   *Separated* refers to legal separation.
   status   *Married* refers to legal marriage. Cohabitation will appear under **living group**.

6. **Living group**   Record the circumstances in which the client normally lives.
   Non-relatives refers to accommodation shared with non-relatives, including flats and non-staffed group homes.
   SSD Unit (staffed) refers to any residential unit/hostel run by the SSD which is staffed.
   Private/voluntary accommodation refers to lodgings, boarding houses, nursing homes, whether private or run by voluntary organizations.

7. **Employment**   *Care of home/family* refers to clients who are normally occupied full-time with unpaid tasks associated with home care and/or child care.

8. **Psychiatric**   *Don't know* refers to where it is not known
   diagnosis   whether a psychiatric diagnosis has been made.

9. **Case status at**   *Other previous contact:* in the case of a client
   referral   previously known to the referral department, enter the number of weeks since the last contact with the client.

Current open case refers to any case or referral under current investigation.

10. **Departmental classification** See local instructions.

11. **Worker** The name will not appear on the carbon sent for processing.

ASW refers to those approved by their local authority.

Working outside normal locality refers to when the worker acts outside the geographical area in which s/he works during normal hours.

12. **Action requested** *Assessment: action not specified* refers to requests for social work assessment where hospital admission is considered to be a possible outcome, but no reference is made to a specific admission section.

MHRT report includes requests for reports to hospital managers.

13. **Outcome** *Advice given: contact* refers to when 'assessment: action not specified' is requested. Face-to-face contact is made with client/family and advice counselling is given.

Advice given: no contact refers to where the advice/counselling is given to referrer/client/family by telephone.

No application: informal in-patient status continued refers to where an informal patient for whom compulsion has been rejected remains informal.

No application: nearest relative application refers to where, after the ASW has declined to make an application, the nearest relative makes an application. Note that the request for a report under S14 will be recorded on a separate form as another piece of work.

No application: alternative care refers to where, in response to a request to admit, the ASW arranges satisfactory care without recourse to admission.

		Aftercare refers to face-to-face client contact after referral.
14.	**Alternatives**	This concerns alternatives to admission, **not** alternatives to the client's current care. Where admission (compulsory or informal) was requested but did not take place, tick the boxes in the 'Used' column corresponding to the arrangements made. If another alternative would have been considered more suitable, or a useful addition to that used, tick that in the 'Required' column. Where admission (compulsory or informal) took place, tick the boxes in the 'Required' column corresponding to the alternative arrangements (**if any**) which would have prevented admission.
15.	**Describe alternatives**	Describe how the alternatives used/required, prevented/could have prevented admission. Give details of alternatives used/required.

December, 1984 SSRG1

APPENDIX 3

Table A3.1 Comparisons between local authority areas
Rates per 100,000 population: requests and outcomes

	All assessments	REQUESTS Assessments for: s.2	s.3	s.4	OUTCOMES Sections 2,3,4	s.2	s.3	s.4
LONDON BOROUGHS								
10	59.3	24.9	9.2	8.0	29.1	17.6	5.5	6.1
11	69.8	16.9	3.4	29.3	27.6	10.7	2.8	14.1
12	104.6	44.3	14.4	9.1	48.0	28.0	14.4	4.8
14	136.6	46.9	16.1	10.7	69.7	41.5	15.4	12.7
15	108.7	55.1	9.4	2.5	39.2	30.3	7.4	1.5
16	31.9	13.5	11.5	6.6	27.4	11.5	9.0	6.9
17	111.5	18.6	13.3	33.6	38.5	16.8	10.2	11.5
18	73.7	39.5	13.0	1.8	44.8	31.2	13.0	0.6
19	92.0	34.4	11.2	20.5	53.9	27.4	10.7	15.8
20	196.1	91.3	34.2	16.3	102.7	63.0	27.7	12.0
22	203.8	39.3	5.5	0.9	25.7	18.8	4.1	2.9
24	140.5	64.3	21.4	19.1	79.4	44.4	19.8	15.1
25	106.5	44.2	17.6	7.0	53.8	29.2	15.6	9.1
London Boroughs	110.8	39.8	13.3	12.7	47.4	27.3	11.4	8.6
METROPOLITAN DISTRICTS								
27	82.0	39.0	20.5	0.0	49.0	29.0	19.5	0.5
28	49.9	25.0	6.2	2.0	25.7	18.7	5.5	1.6
30	48.3	22.4	4.7	2.8	21.6	16.1	3.5	2.0
31	29.3	16.0	2.0	0.0	17.3	14.0	2.7	0.7
32	54.6	38.1	11.6	0.7	45.1	32.1	12.2	0.7
33	109.2	55.1	28.2	10.1	80.2	45.5	26.5	8.1
34	100.1	49.0	10.2	6.8	48.4	33.1	9.8	5.4
35	53.1	26.4	5.2	2.8	23.6	18.8	3.5	1.4
36	77.2	28.2	26.4	12.7	47.3	18.6	21.8	6.8
37	41.2	26.3	4.5	2.4	23.6	18.5	3.6	1.5
40	142.6	13.9	6.9	16.4	29.0	11.0	7.6	9.5
42	112.4	41.0	21.7	16.9	65.2	36.2	19.3	9.7
45	52.7	27.7	12.3	6.6	39.7	25.8	10.6	3.3
47	38.1	6.6	9.3	5.8	16.4	5.3	7.5	3.5
49	52.9	22.6	11.6	7.5	35.0	17.9	10.7	6.4
Met. Districts	65.9	31.6	12.3	5.4	40.3	25.3	11.4	3.6

Table A3.1 Comparisons between local authority areas
Rates per 100,000 population: requests and outcomes (contd.)

	All assessments	REQUESTS Assessments for:			OUTCOMES Sections			
		s.2	s.3	s.4	2,3,4	s.2	s.3	s.4
COUNTY COUNCILS								
1	56.7	18.8	8.4	18.5	36.6	16.6	4.5	12.1
2	51.5	25.2	7.5	6.2	30.5	18.8	5.5	4.6
3	50.7	16.5	11.1	7.3	30.8	13.6	10.8	6.5
4	47.8	29.2	6.4	3.8	30.7	22.6	1.2	2.6
5	35.2	15.3	6.4	1.6	20.3	13.1	5.9	1.4
6	38.9	21.4	5.9	1.0	19.9	13.6	5.6	0.7
7	56.0	15.0	12.7	9.3	31.6	12.5	12.8	6.3
8	47.4	14.1	7.1	7.5	27.6	14.6	6.8	6.2
9	90.2	37.2	11.1	3.9	32.6	21.3	8.0	3.3
26	36.5	19.3	8.5	3.6	24.6	16.0	6.6	2.1
29	46.4	26.3	7.9	2.0	29.1	20.8	6.1	2.2
38	115.6	39.1	16.0	19.7	55.5	25.5	5.7	14.8
46	46.0	17.6	1.0	7.1	25.9	13.3	9.1	3.5
48	53.2	13.7	5.3	12.2	23.8	10.8	4.1	8.9
County Councils								
	52.5	21.7	8.6	7.6	29.8	16.8	7.7	5.4
All Authorities								
	65.3	27.3	10.4	7.8	35.4	20.9	9.3	5.4

Table A3.2 Diversion into alternative care and informal admission

Following assessment for:	Alternative care			Informal admission		
	Section 2	Section 3	Section 4	Section 2	Section 3	Section 4
LONDON BOROUGHS						
10	15.4	12.5	38.1	9.2	16.7	4.8
11	13.3	0	23.1	13.3	16.7	21.2
12	15.9	7.4	5.9	7.3	3.7	23.5
14	5.7	8.3	12.5	12.9	16.7	18.8
15	18.9	15.8	0	20.7	5.3	40.0
16	3.0	0	0	6.1	17.9	0
17	11.9	6.7	18.4	4.8	16.7	35.5
18	11.9	0	0	11.9	0	33.3
19	12.2	0	25.0	5.4	8.3	6.8
20	14.3	1.6	20.0	16.7	9.5	20.0
22	41.9	5.3	0	21.3	5.3	0
24	9.9	7.4	12.5	14.8	7.4	20.8
25	14.8	5.7	0	14.8	2.9	28.6
London Boroughs						
	16.9	5.2	17.8	13.9	9.5	20.9
METROPOLITAN DISTRICTS						
27	9.0	7.3	–	16.7	2.4	–
28	9.4	0	20.0	15.6	12.5	0

Table A3.2 Diversion into alternative care and informal admission
(Contd.)

| | Alternative care | | | Informal admission | | |
| Following assessment for: | | | | | | |
	Section 2	Section 3	Section 4	Section 2	Section 3	Section 4
30	22.8	*0*	*14.3*	12.3	*8.3*	*28.6*
31	4.2	*0*	–	14.6	0	–
32	4.9	0	*0*	10.3	1.5	*0*
33	7.1	0	4.3	11.5	7.8	8.7
34	12.4	0	15.0	18.6	6.7	10.0
35	7.9	6.7	*25.0*	13.2	*13.3*	*12.5*
36	11.3	5.2	10.7	21.0	5.2	25.0
37	5.7	*0*	*25.0*	14.8	*20.0*	*25.0*
40	13.6	*0*	19.2	9.1	*0*	23.1
42	7.6	0	16.3	12.6	11.1	12.2
45	5.1	1.9	25.0	6.0	9.6	14.3
47	*20.0*	4.8	7.7	*6.7*	19.0	*38.5*
49	12.8	5.0	11.5	10.3	0	11.5
Met. Districts	8.6	1.9	14.2	12.8	7.1	15.7
COUNTY COUNCILS						
1	7.5	4.2	10.1	11.3	4.2	15.9
2	13.1	2.4	8.8	12.4	7.3	23.5
3	9.8	0	17.8	12.7	7.2	15.6
4	5.1	3.3	22.2	20.4	6.7	*16.7*
5	10.7	6.4	*8.3*	12.5	2.1	*8.3*
6	14.6	5.6	*16.7*	16.9	11.1	*0*
7	11.1	3.3	10.4	13.9	9.9	22.4
8	11.3	3.2	12.1	4.8	3.2	21.2
9	17.4	3.3	9.5	23.9	20.0	9.5
26	6.0	0	10.0	14.9	13.5	23.3
29	9.5	6.3	15.0	14.5	11.4	5.0
38	8.4	2.6	25.0	16.8	5.1	10.4
46	9.0	4.3	18.4	19.7	10.1	24.5
48	13.0	0	8.7	15.6	16.7	14.5
County Councils	10.4	3.3	12.7	15.5	9.4	16.8
All Authorities	11.3	3.2	14.3	14.3	8.6	17.6

* Italics are used where percentages are based on less than 20 cases

APPENDIX 4

Authority A is the authority we discussed on page 81 with a multi-disciplinary crisis-intervention team. There were in this authority no exceptional community-based mental-health resources but there was a commitment to assessments that were both jointly undertaken and genuinely collaborative. There was also a concern to keep in regular touch with those with known problems resulting from mental disorder and to visit others referred to them during the early phase of periods of stress that might lead to eventual hospitalization. Most of the requests made were for 'not-specified' assessments, though very few of these led to compulsory detention. Otherwise the authority experienced average (section 2) or low bombardment rates and the achievement of high levels of diversion and avoidance for section 2 requests and average diversion of section 3 requests. All the section 4 requests resulted in compulsory detention but there were only three. There was little scope for further prevention according to the social workers but the distinct result of these arrangements and philosophy was a very low proportion of requests concerning section 4, and overall, the lowest rate of detention for its type of authority and one of the lowest in the study.

Authority B, despite high rates of section 2 referral, showed an almost identical pattern of diversion outcome and potential further diversion and a below average overall detention rate. There is within this authority a managerial commitment to realizing as far as possible the Act's intention to create a more positive role for the ASW in decisions about compulsory admission. Detailed expectations of the active consideration of treatment and care outside hospital have been laid down and a small number of ASWs appointed. Very few requests are handled by hospital social workers and the authority's results have been strongly influenced by one community-based generic team who have developed good relationships with the local psychiatric hospital, with whose personnel joint domiciliary visits aimed at prevention are undertaken. They have made it clear they will not agree to section 4 except in dire emergencies and so are rarely asked. They expect more success at preventing admission with clients who are known, which is perhaps more likely in this area because unexceptional levels of child-care work make longer term work with the mentally disordered easier to achieve. Two ASWs were also designated as 'social workers with a special interest in mental health', which meant that approximately 75 per cent of their caseload were mental health cases. Both the area officer in post at the time and an influential senior social worker on the team were particularly interested in that area of the department's work.

Authority C was more representative of a group of authorities that achieved average or slightly above average levels of diversion but were conscious that further detentions, and particularly inappropriate uses of some sections could be avoided. During 1985 they had created a network of community mental-health teams and doubled the number of ASWs. Six teams in one health authority were multidisciplinary and directly involved in admissions to hospital. As a consequence it was felt that both enhanced relationships with health services staff and the extended availability of the expertise of ASWs would result in less inappropriate detention than previously. Authority C's overall volume of requests was average but it had a below average rate of section 4 requests and an above average rate for section 2 requests. Diversion of section 2 requests into alternative care was average but for sections 3 and 4, above average, though there was rather less avoidance of compulsion by means of informal admission. The result of this was that the authority had average outcomes of detention, with relatively few emergency admissions. This may well reflect local emphasis in the training of ASWs on limiting section 4 admissions to strict emergencies and use of section 3 principally with known patients. Even so, there was an awareness of high-potential further diversion of emergency admissions and average/ above-average potential concerning sections 2 and 3. Staff report further success at reducing the use of section 4 since the end of our study.

Authority D was an area with a strong commitment to psychiatric hospitals within the health service with plans during the period of the research to introduce a new hospital. Section 12 doctors were in short supply in the community. All the hospitals had social work teams based there, though shortly after the study ended these workers were reorganized into community mental health teams. Emergency duty cover was difficult to provide because of the large geographical area of the county. Social services staff reported a legacy of numbers of nearest relative applications and frequent use of the emergency section because of the difficulty of getting second medical examinations. One target had been to reduce the high rates of section 4 requests by applying a strict definition of 'emergency' and another was to encourage the use of section 3 rather than section 2 where a patient was well known. In fact in the year of our study it experienced average bombardment levels for all three sections and achieved considerably higher than average diversion of section 3 and 4 requests with average diversion of those concerning section 2, and modest avoidance by means of informal admission. As a result it had average (section 2) or below average outcomes of detention. Social services staff were also keen to establish a more prominent role for community mental health services that did not replicate medical and institutional models on a smaller scale. Progress was slow and few resources available at the time our study ended and the results demonstrated an awareness that there was further potential diversion of all three types of request, were resources available.

Authority E has a higher than average rate of requests for section 4, a high rate for section 2, and a very high rate for section 3. Such high bombardment is not necessarily seen as problematic. Staff in the authority feel it has a strong commitment to mental health services and that one concomitant of a high level of activity might be high levels of requests for compulsion to be applied. The response to these high bombardment rates is below average (section 2) or very low diversion and below average avoidance as well. In consequence, the authority has the second highest overall detention rate of all authorities. Yet social workers saw low potential for any further diversion. Local analysis has identified a significantly higher level of detention within one of the authority's three health districts and two possible explanations have been put forward. First, local reports suggest that this district is further down the path of resettling long-stay patients in the community. If so, it is possible that many will be in need of periodic admission for care and treatment and this would result in higher levels of requests for compulsory admission. Indeed, the district has attracted the suggestion from the MHAC that it may operate a too rapidly turning revolving door. Second, there has been within the district a particular concern to avoid what the MHAC has called *de facto* detention of voluntary patients. A vigorous policy of keeping detained and informal patients comprehensively informed of their rights has followed and may have contributed to a higher level of formal restriction where there was a concern for people's welfare.

Authority F has in some ways a similar profile. It has very high referral rates for sections 2 and 3 and a considerably higher than average rate of emergency requests. Diversion into alternative care is below average for the type of authority for sections 2 and 3, although it is above average for section 4, and there is only average avoidance by means of informal admission. Why this should occur in an authority which is not one of the poorest in terms of resources is not entirely clear. Bombardment rates are slightly inflated by a higher than average level of inappropriate requests, which perhaps concern people about whom little is known. Certainly local analysis has shown that nearly half of all requests concern residents of other authorities and local managers speculate that it may be more difficult to provide alternatives in these circumstances. Another partial explanation for the relatively low diversion figures may lie in shortage of section 12 doctors and the local practice whereby psychiatrists do not undertake domiciliary visits. The characteristics of people referred in this authority are also different from the national picture. Three times as many are homeless and one and a half times as many live alone, yet people with these characteristics are less likely to be detained nationally! Another point to emerge from closer scrutiny of this particular authority's results is that results are not uniform across the authority. The relatively low-diversion figures are heavily influenced by the practice of one hospital team and community based teams achieve similar results to those in other authorities.

211

None the less the final outcome is very high levels of detention for each section and the highest overall detention rate in the study. Furthermore, social workers saw low potential across the board for significant further prevention.

APPENDIX 5

CHARACTERISTICS OF PEOPLE REFERRED DURING THE STUDY PERIOD

Table A5.1 Age/gender

	<24	25–34	35–44	45–54	55–64	65–74	75–84	85+	Total
Male	822	1,011	797	518	394	295	208	44	4,089
%	58.3	53.3	45.8	40.5	33.8	31.9	27.7	19.5	
Female	589	887	948	761	774	632	542	182	5,315
%	41.7	46.7	54.3	59.5	66.3	68.2	72.3	80.5	
Total	1,411	1,898	1,745	1,279	1,168	927	750	226	9,404

Table A5.2 Marital status/gender

	Male		Female	
	No.	%	No.	%
Single	2,144	55.8	1,455	28.6
Married	943	24.5	1,734	34.1
Separated	186	4.8	242	4.8
Widowed	210	5.5	1,028	20.2
Divorced	362	9.4	631	12.4

Table A5.3 Living group/gender

	Male		Female	
	No.	%	No.	%
Alone	1,184	30.0	1,742	33.4
Spouse/cohab. with or without children	961	24.3	1,758	33.7
Children only	60	1.5	458	8.8
Parents/parents and siblings	1,033	26.2	585	11.2
Other family	137	3.6	136	2.6
Non-relatives	149	3.8	121	2.3
Institution	328	8.3	332	6.4
Other	101	2.6	89	1.7

Table A5.4 Employment status/gender

	Male		Female	
	No	%	No	%
Full-time employment	597	15.7	295	5.9
Full-time care of home/ family	12	0.3	982	19.5
Part-time employment	70	1.8	220	4.4
Unemployed	2,332	61.2	1,871	37.2
Retired	601	15.8	1,531	30.4
Student	72	1.9	46	0.9
Other	125	3.3	91	1.8

Table A5.5 Housing/gender

	Male		Female	
	No.	%	No.	%
Owner-occupied	1,190	33.2	1,845	39.0
Private rented	294	8.2	362	7.6
Council	1,335	37.3	1,952	41.2
Lodgings	208	5.8	133	2.8
Homeless	223	6.2	139	2.9
Other	329	9.2	307	6.5

Table A5.6 Age/gender/ethnic group (all authorities)

| | White | | Afro-Caribbean | | Asian | |
	Male	Female	Male	Female	Male	Female
<24	595	456	120	65	40	33
25–34	800	723	92	62	61	44
35–44	699	831	29	42	34	34
45–54	458	669	27	43	18	26
55–64	358	727	14	15	8	10
65–74	280	608	1	3	4	3
75–84	201	528	1	0	1	3
85+	44	181	0	0	0	0
Total	3,435	4,723	284	230	166	153

Table A5.7 Age/gender/psychiatric diagnosis (where given)

| | <24 | | 25–34 | | 35–44 | | 45–54 | | 55–64 | | 65+ | |
	M	F	M	F	M	F	M	F	M	F	M	F
Schizophrenia	211	94	288	182	246	216	132	189	81	159	49	152
Affective psychosis	36	30	68	83	83	124	57	118	39	98	33	87
Other psychosis	45	38	42	56	19	47	19	30	16	21	6	33
Dementia	0	0	3	1	0	2	2	2	12	11	100	226
Neurotic disorder	9	23	19	29	19	25	11	24	15	28	13	214
Depression	23	50	43	81	47	93	39	98	64	127	84	22
Personality disorder	27	23	41	32	22	30	14	11	3	9	3	8
Mental handicap	13	6	11	16	7	5	5	2	3	3	1	1
Non-specific mental illness	15	10	11	21	21	6	10	7	6	6	5	12
Other	12	14	22	10	30	19	14	13	9	13	18	12

APPENDIX 6

COMPARATIVE OUTCOMES OF ASSESSMENTS FOR DIFFERENT POPULATION SUB-GROUPS

Table A6.1 Admission or alternative care/population subgroup

	Compulsory admission No.	%	Informal admission No.	%	Alternative care No.	%
All men	2,424	50.3	878	18.2	856	17.8
All women	3,351	52.0	1,158	18.0	1217	18.9
All people living alone	1,702	46.9	650	17.9	755	20.8
All people living in NHS, SSD, or P & V	330	51.5	111	17.3	120	18.7
Single men living with parents	659	58.3	160	14.2	193	17.1
Single women living with parents	330	62.6	75	14.2	72	13.7
Men under 35	1,126	53.4	363	17.2	339	16.0
Women under 35	926	53.2	327	18.8	287	16.5
Men 35–64	965	49.9	355	18.4	355	18.4
Women 35–64	1,626	54.3	540	18.0	516	17.2
Men under 55 living with spouse/cohab. with or without children	365	52.9	125	18.1	111	16.1
Women under 55 living with spouse/cohab. with or without children	800	55.6	276	19.2	232	16.1
Afro-Caribbean men	229	62.1	40	10.8	49	13.3
Afro-Caribbean women	185	60.5	45	14.7	42	13.7
White men	1,998	49.4	783	19.4	739	18.3
White women	2,960	51.7	1,055	18.4	1,094	19.1
Asian men	107	57.5	22	11.8	32	17.2
Asian women	100	52.6	34	17.9	40	21.1
Diagnosis – men schizophrenia	812	62.8	183	14.1	180	13.9
Diagnosis – women schizophrenia	819	63.9	201	15.7	175	13.7

Table A6.2 Comparative potential diversion rates for different population subgroups

(percentage of those admitted where this was considered avoidable)

All men	28.5	Men under 55 living with spouse/cohabitee	27.9
All women	28.6		
All people living alone	29.6	Women under 55 living with spouse/cohabitee	27.2
Men living in residential accommodation	34.0	Afro-Caribbean men	25.7
Women living in residential accommodation	23.8	Afro-Caribbean women	28.3
		White men	29.2
Single men living with parents	28.3	White women	28.5
Single women living with parents	26.9	Asian men	26.4
Men under 35	28.7	Asian women	31.3
Women under 35	29.1	Diagnosis schizophrenia men	27.0
Men 35–64	27.3	Diagnosis schizophrenia women	26.6
Women 35–64	27.7		

Table A6.3 Alternatives used to prevent admission

	All men	All women	Afro-Caribbean men	Afro-Caribbean women	Asian men	Asian women
Family	275	474	20	14	8	20
support	39.5	47.4	41.7	42.4	30.8	55.6
Social work	355	525	24	20	12	23
	51.0	52.5	50.0	60.6	46.2	63.9
GP	260	387	17	13	7	9
	37.4	38.7	35.4	39.4	26.9	25.0
Day care	63	65	1	1	1	0
	9.1	6.5	2.1	3.0	3.8	0
Day hospital	45	66	1	0	1	0
	6.5	6.6	2.1	0	3.8	0
Residential care	54	82	2	4	1	0
	7.8	8.2	4.2	12.1	3.8	0
O/P	204	253	15	11	7	9
	29.3	25.3	31.3	33.3	26.9	25.0
Domiciliary	36	141	1	2	0	0
support	5.2	14.1	2.1	6.1	0	0
CPN	120	251	7	11	7	13
	17.2	25.1	14.6	33.3	26.9	36.1
Crisis int.	50	83	3	5	2	5
	7.2	8.3	6.3	15.2	7.7	13.9
Vol. help	43	48	3	9	1	0
	6.2	4.8	6.3	27.3	3.8	0
Other	95	145	7	4	3	4
	13.6	14.5	14.6	12.1	11.5	11.1
Total cases in which alternatives used	696	1,000	48	33	26	36

Note: The first line for each category is a number, while the second indicates a percentage.

218

REFERENCES

Abrams, M.(1980) *Beyond Three Score Years and Ten: A Second Report on a Survey of the Elderly*, Mitcham: Age Concern.

Anderson-Ford, D. and Halsey, M.D. (1984) *Mental Health Law and Practice for Social Workers*, London: Butterworth.

Anon (1984) Letter to the *British Medical Journal*, 289(6457):1542.

Anwar, M. (1986) 'Young Asians between Two Cultures', in V. Coombe and A. Little (eds) *Race and Social Work, A Guide to Training*, London: Tavistock.

Audit Commission (1986) *Making a Reality of Community Care*, London: HMSO.

Bachrach, L. (1977) *Deinstitutionalization: An Analytical Review and Sociological Perspective*, Rockville: National Institute of Mental Health.

Bailey, S. (1987) 'A mental health centre: the user's view in its evaluation', *Social Services Research*, (3): 25–38.

Banton, R., Clifford, P., Frosh S., Lousada, J., and Rosenthal, J. (1985) *The Politics of Mental Health*, Basingstoke: Macmillan.

Barker, I. and Peck, E. (1987) *Power in Strange Places: User Empowerment in Mental Health Services*, London: Good Practices in Mental Health.

Barnes, M. (1987) 'The SSRG Project "Monitoring the Mental Health Act 1983" as a model of collaborative research', in R. Hugman and P. Huxley (eds) *Working Together: Research, Practice and Education in Social Work*, University of Lancaster: Department of Social Administration.

Barnes, M. and Prior, D. (1984) *Monitoring the Impact of the Mental Health Act 1983*, L.B.Hounslow Social Services Department.

Barnes, M., Bowl, R., and Fisher, M. (1986) 'The Mental Health Act 1983 and Social Services', *Research, Policy and Planning*, 4 (1 /2):1–7.

Barrett, M. and McIntosh, M. (1982) *The Anti-social Family*, London: Verso.

Baruch, G., and Treacher, A. (1978) *Psychiatry Observed*, London: Routledge & Kegan Paul.

Bean, P. (1975) 'The Mental Health Act 1959: some issues concerning rule enforcement', *British Journal of Law and Society*, 2:225–35.

Bean, P. (1980) *Compulsory Admissions to Mental Hospitals*, Chichester: John Wiley.

Bean, P. (1987) 'The Mental Health Act 1983: An overview', in M. Brenton and C. Ungerson (eds) *The Year Book of Social Policy 1986–87*, Harlow: Longman.

Birmingham City Council (1987) *Community Care Special Action Project*, Project Journal, 1st edn.

Black, J., Bowl, R., Burns, D., Critcher, C., Grant, G., and Stockford, R. (1983) *Social Work in Context*, London: Tavistock.

Bleicher, B. (1967) ' Compulsory community care for the mentally ill', *Cleveland Law Review*, 16: 93–115.

Booth, T., Melotte, C., Phillips, D., Pritlove, J., Barritt, A., and Lightup, R. (1985) 'Psychiatric crises in the community: collaboration and the 1983 Mental Health Act', in G. Horobin (ed.) *Responding to Mental Illness, Research Highlights in Social Work*, London: Kogan Page.

Bott, E. (1976) 'Hospital and society', *British Journal of Medical Psychology*, 49: 97–140.

Bowl, R. (1978) *Social Problems in a New Town-The Response of the Social Services Department*, Birmingham: Birmingham University Social Services Unit.

Bowl, R. (1986) 'Social work with old people', in C. Phillipson and A. Walker (eds) *Ageing and Social Policy: A Critical Assessment*, Aldershot: Gower.

Bowl, R., Barnes, M., and Fisher, M. (1987) 'A real alternative', *Community Care*, 2 July, pp. 26–8.

Braun, P., Kochansky, G., Shapiro, R., Greenberg, S., Gudeman, J., Johnson, S., and Shore, M. (1981) 'Overview: deinstitutionalization of psychiatric patients, a critical review of outcome studies'. *Amercian Journal of Psychiatry*, 138(6): 736–49.

Bravington, J. and Majid, A. (1986) 'Psychiatric services for ethnic minority groups', in J.L. Cox (ed.) *Transcultural Psychiatry*, London: Croom Helm.

Broverman, D., Clarkson, F., Rosenkrantz, P., Vogel, S., and Broverman, I. (1970) 'Sex-role stereotype and clinical judgements of mental health', *Journal of Consulting and Clinical Psychology*, 34: 1–7.

Brown, C. (1984) *Black and White Britain: The Third PSI Report*, London: Heinemann.

Brown, G.W. and Harris, T. (1978) *Social Origins of Depression: A Study of Psychiatric Disorder in Women*, London: Tavistock.

Brown, M. (1985) *Introduction to Social Administration in Britain*, London: Hutchinson.

Brown, P. (1979) 'The transfer of care: US mental health policy since World War II', *International Journal of Health Services*, 9 (4): 645–62.

Brown, P. (1985) 'The mental patients' rights movement and mental health institutional change', in P. Brown (ed.) *Mental Health Care and Social Policy*, London: Routledge & Kegan Paul.

Brown, R. (1983) 'No need for stage fright', *Community Care*, 9 June, pp.14–17.

Burke, A.W. (1986) 'Racism, prejudice and mental illness', in J.L. Cox (ed.) *Transcultural Psychiatry*, London: Croom Helm.

Butler, T. (1985) *Mental Health, Social Policy and the Law*, London: Macmillan.

Campbell, B. (1984) *Wigan Pier Revisted. Poverty and Politics in the 80s*, London: Virago.

Carstairs, G.M. and Kapur, R.C. (1976) *The Great Universe of Kota: Stress Charge and Mental Disorder in an Indian Village*, London: Hogarth Press.

Castel, F., Castel, R., and Lovell, A. (1982) *The Psychiatric Society*, New York: Columbia University Press.

CCETSW (1987a) Paper 19.19, *Regulations and Guidance for the training of social workers to be considered for approval in England and Wales under the MHA 1983*, January.

CCETSW (1987b) *Third Report of Examinations Board to Council*, July.

Cheetham, J. (1981) *Social Work Services for Ethnic Minorities in Britain and the USA*, London: DHSS.

Christian, L. (1985) *Approved Social Work?* Norwich: UEA/Social Work Today Monograph Series.

CIPFA (1987) *Personal Social Services Statistics Actuals 1985–86*, London: The Chartered Institute of Public Finance and Accountancy.

Clare, A. (1976) *Psychiatry in Dissent*, London: Tavistock.

Cochrane, R. (1983) *The Social Creation of Mental Illness*, London: Longman.

Cochrane, R. and Stopes-Roe, M. (1981) 'Women, marriage, employment and mental health', *British Journal of Psychiatry*, 139: 373–81.

Cocozza, J. and Steadman, H. (1978) 'Prediction in psychiatry: an example of misplaced confidence in experts', *Social Problems*, 25 (3): 265–76.

Cohen, C. and Sokolovsky, J. (1978) 'Schizophrenia and social networks; ex-patients in the inner city', *Schizophrenia Bulletin*, 4: 546–60.

Cohen, J. and Fisher, M. (1987) 'Recognition of mental health problems by doctors and social workers', *Practice*, 1 (3): 225–40.

Corney, R. and Briscoe, M. (1977) 'Social workers and their clients: a comparison between primary health care and local authority settings', *Journal of the Royal College of General Practitioners*, 27: 295–301.

Coxall, J.A. (1987) An investigation of perceptions of the relationship between unemployment and psychological ill health, unpublished individual research project report, Newcastle upon Tyne Polytechnic: Faculty of Community and Social Studies.

Crine, A. (1983) 'Controversy was his shadow', *Community Care*, 27 January, pp. 12–13.

Dale, J. and Foster, P. (1986) *Feminists and State Welfare*, London: Routledge & Kegan Paul.

Davies, B. (1968) *Social Needs and Resources in Local Services*, London: Michael Joseph.

Davis, A. (1984) 'Residential care', in M.R. Olsen (ed.) *Social Work and Mental Health, A Guide for the Approved Social Worker*, London: Tavistock.

Davis, A., Llewellyn, S., and Parry, G. (1985) 'Women and mental health: towards an understanding', in E. Brook and A. Davis (eds) *Women, The Family and Social Work*, London: Tavistock.

Dawson, H. (1972) 'Reasons for compulsory admission', in J. Wing and A. Hailey (eds) *Evaluating a Community Psychiatric Service*, Oxford: Oxford University Press.

DHSS (1975) *Better Services for the Mentally Ill*, Command 6233, London: HMSO.

DHSS (1978) *A Review of the Mental Health Act 1959*, Command 7320, London: HMSO.

DHSS (1981) *Reform of the Mental Health Legislation*, Command 8405, London: HMSO.

DHSS (1986) Unpublished statistics from the Mental Health Enquiry, 1985.

DHSS (1987) Unpublished statistics from the Mental Health Enquiry, 1986.

Dick, D. H. (1981) 'The medical contribution to the management of mental illness services', *Bulletin of the Royal College of Psychiatrists*, 5: 119–20.

Dooher, I. (1989) 'Research note; guardianship under the Mental Health Act 1983, practice in Leicestershire', *British Journal of Social Work*, 19 (2).

Durrant, P. (1983) 'Mental Handicap – In on the Act', *Community Care*, 15 December, 19–21.

Edwards, S. and Huxley, P. (1985) 'A matter of considerable concern', *Community Care*, 28 November, pp. 14–16.

Emerson, R. and Pollner, M. (1975) 'Dirty work designations; their features and consequences in a psychiatric setting', *Social Problems*, 23: 243–54.

Erickson, G. (1976) 'Personal networks and mental illness', doctoral dissertation, University of York.

Fabrikant, B. (1974) 'The psychotherapist and the female patient: perceptions and change', in V. Franks and V. Burtle (eds), *Women in Therapy*, New York: Bruner/Mazel.

Fagin, L. (1981) *Unemployment and Health in Families*, London: DHSS.

Fernando, S. (1986) 'Depression in ethnic minorities', in J.L. Cox (ed.)

Transcultural Psychiatry, London: Croom Helm.

Finch, J. and Groves, D. (1985) 'Old girl, old boy: gender divisions in social work with the elderly', in E. Brook and A. Davis (eds) *Women, the Family and Social Work*, London: Tavistock.

Fisher, M. (1983) 'Mental health legislation and local authority policy', *Research, Policy and Planning* 1(2): 26–8.

Fisher, M. (1988) 'Guardianship under the Mental Health Act 1983: a review', *Journal of Social Welfare Law*, 5: 316-27.

Fisher, M., Barnes, M., and Bowl, R.(1987) 'Monitoring the Mental Health Act 1983; implications for policy and practice', *Research,Policy and Planning* 5(1): 1–8.

Fisher, M., Newton, C., and Sainsbury, E. (1984) *Mental Health Social Work Observed*, London: George Allen & Unwin.

Fransella, F. and Frost, K. (1977) *On Being a Woman*, London: Tavistock.

Gilleard, C. (1985) 'The psychogeriatric patient and the family', in G. Horobin (ed.) *Responding to Mental Illness, Research Highlights in Social Work, 11*, London: Kogan Page.

GLC (1985) 'I Wanted a Safe Place', in *GLC Women's Committee Bulletin*, Issue 23, London: GLC.

Goldberg, D. and Huxley, P. (1980) *Mental Illness in the Community*, London: Tavistock.

Gostin, L. (1975) *A Human Condition, vol 1*, London: MIND.

Gostin, L. (1983) *A Practical Guide to Mental Health Law*, London: MIND.

Gostin, L. (1986) *Mental Health Services, Law and Practice*, London: Shaw.

Gray, B. and Isaacs, B. (1979) *Care of the Elderly Mentally Infirm*, London: Tavistock.

Greenley, J. (1979) ' Family symptom tolerance and rehospitalisation experiences of psychiatric patients', *Research in Community and Mental Health* 1: 357–86.

Griffiths, R. (1988) *Community Care: Agenda for Action*, London: HMSO/DHSS.

Gunn, M.J. (1986) 'Mental Health Act guardianship; where now?', *Journal of Social Welfare Law* (5): 145–52.

Hale, J. (1983) 'Feminism and social work practice', in B. Jordan and N. Parton (eds) *The Political Dimensions of Social Work*, Oxford: Blackwell.

Hammer, M., Makiesky-Barrow, S., and Gutwirth, L. (1978) 'Social networks and schizophrenia', *Schizophrenia Bulletin* 4: 522–45.

Hayes, J. and Nutman, P. (1981) *Understanding the Unemployed*, London: Tavistock.

Henley, A. (1986) 'The Asian Community in Britain', in V. Coombe and A. Little (eds) *Race and Social Work. A Guide to Training*, London: Tavistock.

Hey, A. (1985) 'Hard Act to follow?' *Social Work Today*, 4 February: 15–17.

Hitch, P. and Clegg, P. (1980) 'Modes of referral of overseas immigrant and native born first admissions to psychiatric hospital', *Social Sciences and Medicine*, 14A: 369–74.

Hoggett, B. (1984) *Mental Health Law*, (2nd edn), London: Sweet & Maxwell.

Hudson, B. (1982) *Social Work with Psychiatric Patients*, London: Macmillan.

Husband, C. (1986) 'Racism, prejudice and social policy'. in V. Coombe and A. Little (eds) *Race and Social Work, A Guide to Training*, London: Tavistock.

Huxley, P. and Fitzpatrick, R. (1984) 'The probable extent of minor mental illness in the adult clients of social workers: a research note', *British Journal of Social Work*, 14: 67–73.

Ineichen, B., Harrison, G., and Morgan, H.G. (1984) 'Psychiatric hospital admissions in Bristol, I, geographical or ethnic factors', *British Journal of Psychiatry* 150: 505–12.

Isaacs, B., Minty, E., and Morrison, R. (1986) 'Children in care – the association with mental disorder in the parents', *British Journal of Social Work*, 16: 325–39.

Jackson, N. (1983) 'Getting our Act together', *Community Care* 9 June, pp. 14–17.

Jahoda, M. (1958) *Current Concepts of Positive Mental Health*, New York: Basic Books.

Jones, K. (1972) *A History of the Mental Health Services*, London: Routledge & Kegan Paul.

Jones, K. and Poletti, A. (1985) 'Understanding the Italian experience', *British Journal of Psychiatry*, (146): 341–7, April.

Jones, K., Brown, J., and Bradshaw, J. (1978) *Issues in Social Policy*, London: Routledge & Kegan Paul.

Jones, L. and Cochrane, R. (1981) 'Stereotypes of mental illness: a test of the labelling hypothesis', *International Journal of Social Psychiatry* 27: 99–107.

Kay, D.W.K. (1963) 'Late paraphrenia and its bearing on the aetiology of schizophrenia', *Acta Psychiatrica Scandinavica* 39: 159–69.

Kiesler, C. (1982) 'Mental Hospitals and alternative care: noninstitutionalisation as potential public policy', *American Psychologist* 37 (4): 349–60.

Kittrie, N. (1971) *The Right To Be Different; Deviance and Enforced Therapy*, Baltimore: Johns Hopkins Press.

Lemert, E. (1962) 'Paranoia and the dynamics of exclusion', in P. Spitzer, N. Denzin (eds) *The Mental Patient: Studies in the Sociology of Deviance*, New York: McGraw-Hill.

Leonard, P. (1984) *Personality and Ideology*, London: Macmillan.

Lewando-Hundt, G. and Grant, L. (1987) 'Studies of black elders – an exercise in window dressing or the groundwork for widening provision', *Social Services Research* (5 & 6): 1–9.

Littlewood, R. and Lipsedge, M. (1982) *Aliens and Alienists, Ethnic Minorities and Psychiatry*, Harmandsworth: Penguin.

Lu, Yi-Chuang (1985) 'The collective approach to psychiatric practice in the Peoples' Republic of China', in P. Brown (ed.) *Mental Health Care and Social Policy*, London: Routledge & Kegan Paul.

MacIntyre, S. and Oldman, D. (1977) 'Coping with migraine', in A. Davis and G. Horobin (eds) *Medical Encounters*, London: Croom Helm, p. 62; and in J. Dale and P. Foster (eds) *Feminists and State Welfare*, London: Routledge & Kegan Paul, p. 94 (1986).

Malik, F. (n.d.), *Asian Women and Mental Health or Mental Ill-Health*, Southwark: Asia/Asian Women's Aid.

Maple, N. A. (1988) 'Cognitive analytic therapy as part of the social work service provided by a social services area team', *Social Services Research* (2): 18–29.

Martin, F. M. (1984) *Between the Acts: Community Mental Health Services 1959–1983*, London: Nuffield Provincial Hospital Trust.

McAusland, T. (1985) *Planning and Monitoring Community Mental Health Centres*, London: Kings Fund.

McKinlay, J. (1973) 'Social networks, lay consultation and help-seeking behaviour', *Social Forces* 51 (3): 275–80.

Mental Health Act Commission (1985) *Mental Health Act 1983: Section 118, Draft Code of Practice*, London: Mental Health Division, DHSS.

Mental Health Act Commission (1987) *Second Biennial Report*, 1985–87, London: HMSO.

Mezzina, R., Canosa, R., Vlissides, D., Jenner, F., and Hardy, G. (1986) 'The psychiatric reform in Italy', Trieste: unpublished paper.

Mill, J. (1859) *On Liberty*.

Miller, R. (1982) 'The least restrictive alternative; hidden meanings and agendas', *Community Mental Health Journal* 18 (1): 46–55.

Newton, C. (1988) *Lifestory: A Training Exercise for Approved Social Workers*, University of Birmingham: Social Services Research Group.

Olsen, M.R. (ed.) (1984) *Social Work and Mental Health*, London: Tavistock.

Pattinson, E. (1975) 'A psychosocial kinship model for family therapy', *American Journal of Psychiatry* 132: 369–409.

Peace, S. (1986) 'The forgotten female: social policy and older women', in C. Phillipson and A. Walker (eds) *Ageing and Social Policy: A Critical Assessment*, Aldershot: Gower.

Peay, J. (1982) 'Mental Health Review Tribunals and the Mental Health (Amendment) Act' *Criminal Law Review* December, pp.794–808.

Percy Commission (1957) *Report of the Committee on the Law Relating to Mental Illness and Mental Deficiency* 1954–7, London: HMSO.

Plank, D. (1983) 'Mental Health Act 1983: Memorandum of guidance and information from the Director of Social Services', L.B.Hounslow: Social Services Department.

Ramon, S. (1983) 'Psichiatrica Democratica: a case study of an Italian community mental health service' *International Journal of Health Services* 2: 307–24.

Ramon, S. (1988) 'Italian Democratic Psychiatry Ten Years On', *Open Mind* (33): 12–14.

Revill, M.G. (1982) Letter to *the Lancet* 1: 909.

Rickards, C., Gildersleeve, C., and Fitzgerald, R. (1976) 'The health of clients of a social services department', *Journal of the Royal College of General Practitioners* 26: 237–43.

Ritchie, J., Morrisey, C., and Ward, K. (1988) *Keeping in Touch with the Talking. The Community Care Needs of People with Mental Illness,* Birmingham: Community Care Special Action Project, Social and Community Planning Research.

Rogers, A. and Faulkner, A. (1987) *A Place of Safety,* London: MIND.

Rosenhan, D. (1973) 'On being sane in insane places', *Science* 179: 250–8.

Roth, R. and Lerner, J. (1974) 'Sex-based discrimination in the mental institutionalization of women', *California Law Review* 62: 789–815.

Royal College of Psychiatrists (1979) *Bulletin of the Royal College of Psychiatrists,* April.

Satyamurti, C. (1979) 'Care and control in local authority social work', in N. Parry, M. Rustin, and C. Satyamurti (eds) *Social Work, Welfare and the State,* London: Edward Arnold.

Scheid-Cook, T. (1987) 'Commitment of the mentally ill to out-patient treatment', *Community Mental Health Journal* 23 (3): 173–82.

Schwarz, L. (1974) 'Litigating the right to treatment', *Hospital and Community Psychiatry* 25: 460–3.

Scott, R. and Ashworth, P. (1967) 'Closure at first schizophrenic breakdown: a family study', *British Journal of Medical Psychology* 40: 109–45.

Scull, A. (1977) *Decarceration: Community Treatment and the Deviant: a Radical View,* Englewood Cliffs, New Jersey: Prentice Hall.

Seebohm, F. (1968) *Report of the Committee on Local Authority and Allied Personal Social Services,* London: HMSO.

Seligman, M.E.P. (1975) *Helplessness: On Depression, Development and Death,* San Francisco: W.H. Freeman.

Shapland, J. and Williams, T. (1983) 'Legalism revived: new mental health legislation in England', *International Journal of Law and Psychiatry* 6: 351–69.

Showalter, E. (1987) *The Female Malady, Women, Madness and English Culture 1830–1980,* London: Virago.

Stein, L. and Test, M. (1980) 'Alternative to mental hospital treatment', *Archives of General Psychiatry* 37: 392–7.

Stimson, G. and Webb, B. (1975) *Going to See a Doctor*, London: Routledge & Kegan Paul.

Szasz, T. (1974) *Law, Liberty and Psychiatry*, London: Routledge & Kegan Paul.

Szmuckler, G.I., Bird, A.S., and Button, E.J. (1981) 'Compulsory admissions in a London borough: I. Social and clinical features and follow-up', *Psychological Medicine* 11: 617–36.

Tantam, D. (1985) 'Alternatives to psychiatric hospitalisation', *British Journal of Psychiatry* 146: 1–4.

Taylor, R. and Huxley, P. (1984) 'Social networks and support in social work', *Social Work Education* 3 (2): 25–9.

Tolsdorf, C. (1976) 'Social networks support and coping; an exploratory study', *Family Process* 15: 407–18.

Tonkin, B. (1987) 'Black and blue', *Community Care,* 14 May, pp. 18–20.

Unsworth, C. (1979) 'The balance of law, medicine and social work in mental health legislation 1889–1959', in N. Parry, M. Rustin, and C. Satyamurti (eds), *Social Work, Welfare and the State,* London: Edward Arnold.

Vaughan, C. and Leff, J. (1976) ' The influence of family life and social factors on the course of psychiatric illness', *British Journal of Psychiatry* 129: 125–37.

Warner, A. (1987) 'The quality of life for elderly people living in Birmingham's residential homes'. *Social Services Research* (3): 11–23.

Williams, T. (1988) 'Not just a rubber stamp', *Community Care,* 7 January, pp. 22–3.

Wing, J. (1978) *Reasoning about Madness,* Oxford: Oxford University Press.

Wright, P. (1988) 'Mental Health Act 1983 regional conference on refresher training for approved social workers. Background notes for participants, CCETSW, Rugby Region.

Zola, I. (1972) 'Studying the decision to see a doctor: review, critique and corrective', *Advances in Psychosomatic Medicine* 8: 216–36.

NAME INDEX

SUBJECT INDEX

231